AF578446

Murder at Emerald Meadow

Det. Rick Gordon was able to piece out how two murders were accomplished at a place where there were a hundred people milling around and no one noticed. What was behind it? What made it so suddenly imperative that these two were killed?

One lived the lifestyle that could bring her into such a situation. One did not.

Murder at Emerald Meadow

© 2014 by C. D. Moulton

all rights reserved: no part of this publication may be reproduced or transmitted in any form or by any means, electronic or mechanical, including photocopy, recording, or any information retrieval system, without permission in writing from the copyright holder/publisher, except in the case of brief quotations embodied in critical articles or reviews.

This is a work of fiction. Any resemblance to actual persons or events is purely coincidental

Contents

About the author

CD Moulton has traveled extensively over much of the world both in the music business, where he was a rock guitarist, songwriter and arranger and in an import/export business. He has been everything from a bar owner to auto salvage (junkyard) manager, longshoreman to high steel worker, orchid grower to landscaper, tropical fish farmer to commercial fisherman. He started writing books in 1983 and has published more than 350 books as of January 1, 2023. His most popular books to date are about research with orchids, though much of his science fiction and fantasy work has proven popular. He wrote the CD Grimes, PI series, and the Det. Nick Storie series, Clint Faraday series, and many other works.

He now resides in Gualaca, Chiriqui, Panamá, where he writes books, plays music with friends, does research with orchids and medicinal plants. He has lately become involved in fighting for the rights of the indigenous people, who are among his closest friends, and in fighting the extreme corruption in the courts and police in Panamá.

He offers the free e-book, *Fading Paradise*, that explains what he has been through because of the corruption.

CD is the discoverer of the Chadam Protocol for curing cancer.

Facebook page Ambrosia peruviana for cancer.

Popular Place

Ginger Wells looked around the Emerald Meadow picnic spot as she climbed down from Gladiator, her favorite riding horse. It was only ten o'clock, but there were already fifty or more people around.

That wasn't many for the size of the meadow. It was more than a hundred acres.

She walked Gladiator across to the little oak tree at the edge of the glen and tied him where he could graze on the tender thick grass just past the public area.

Ginger's father owned the whole area. He had made the picnic meadow as a gift to the people of Greenbriar, the town of eight thousand people just a mile and a half away. It would always be open for their use so long as they kept it clean.

Ginger was a pretty girl, just eighteen last month. She was popular.

Her father and mother were strict. She was pursued by several of the men from the area, but Ginger was warned very often that most of them were after her for the money her parents had. Don't be fooled into thinking some appealing young man fell in love with her at first sight or anything so silly. That was crap from romance novels.

Quite as what could be expected, this resulted in her

sneaking away to meet men. She was going to meet Luke Hopkins here in a few minutes. He was perfect! He was everything her parents detested.

Truth be told, she wouldn't give him a second look if they trusted her.

Well, look. He was sorta handsome and had a great body. He wasn't her type. Mentally. He was all for himself. Thought he was god's gift to women. He was everything she was warned to avoid since she was eight or nine years old.

A little voice said, "Which me coming here to meet him shows was on the money."

Luke Hopkins checked out his hair in the left rear view. The thick mop of mahogany hair was about where he wanted it. Molded to best show off his facial features, which weren't all that bad to begin with.

He started the big classic Harley and swung out onto the road.

What the hell was with Ginger? He knew she didn't really care that much about him. She thought he was after money. She didn't know he had as much as he wanted. He'd inherited more than two hundred thousand from his weird uncle, the one who was killed by those two hustler punks he was screwing.

All he was after was getting into her panties. She was sort of the prize among his friends.

Truth be told, he wasn't really that into her for even that.

He didn't make it any secret that was what he was

after. That seemed to turn her on even more.

I wasn't like he had anything else to do today.

Janet Fields ran into the bedroom for her eye kit. She was in too much of a hurry. Slow down or you'll never be ready!

She couldn't wear that blouse with those pants! She ran into the bedroom to get a tee shirt that would go better. It would also show off her boobs, which were her best feature – for this.

Phil would be here any minute and she wasn't half ready! Why couldn't she make up her mind?

Sneakers or flip-flops or shoes?

Jeans and tee shirt. Flip-flops. Be casual.

Where was her medallion? Should she wear it or the little heart?

Jeans, stupid! The medallion!

Where was her cellular? Why couldn't she get organized for one thing in her life?

Right there on the dresser. Now the rings ... no. Not with the other.

Which belt? Is that him? I have to go, so this had better be enough!

She ran out to the waiting car.

Oh, shit! That Nick person was there. Make the best of it! Why did Phil even speak to such as him? Everyone said he was a bum and hustler. She knew he smoked marijuana. She had seen him light up what they called a token or something at Wanda's party.

Phil tossed a package into the console and told Nick

to get in back. He wasn't on a date with him!

Nick got in back. She smiled and got in the car. They headed for the meadow.

Ralph Manners sighed and decided to just shave it all off. He had tried to grow a beard and mustache, but it was little patchy pieces of fuzz. He had that slow thin growth since he was fourteen. Five years later it hadn't changed.

He sighed again. He had to do something to put him aside from the norm. He was pathetically blah. There were ten of him on any block downtown. He was so average he could puke. Average looks, average body, average outlook.

Just fucking average! In everything!

He was told all his life that every person was unique. There was something that was special to everyone, something they excelled at. It could take years to find out what it was.

He had been looking for "What it was" for five years. He still didn't have a hint.

Well, go to the meadow and mingle a bit. He had a few friends who would be there.

He did have a few people who he got along with very well. They sort of meshed. They were also average, though Shirley had a good voice – but she was embarrassed when people asked her to sing.

He knew what that was like. He played the guitar and sang a bit, himself. He was average at playing the guitar and less at singing. Most of what he sang was sing-along. He supposed his voice was good as back-up.

The one thing he sometimes thought he was good at was writing songs. People seemed to like them, but not when he sang them. "Rockin Angels" was a local group that was popular in the bars and at parties. He wrote a thing he called *After the Blues Set In* that they were offered a contract to perform for a recording company. Also local. It wasn't the kind of thing he usually wrote, but he was in a depressed kind of mood and wrote it while Gerry was there. Gerry was lead singer for the group and had loved it. He had a Johnny Cash kind of voice and did it in that style. It was a big hit for them since the first time they did it. He wrote some more for them that were ... average.

The recording was to be released on a CD Monday. Tomorrow. He wrote another on that CD. Maybe it would sell enough that he would actually get ten bucks in royalties!

This wasn't a good way to start a day at the meadow.

He picked up his guitar and went out front to wait for Annette to come by in her Hyundai. She was taking him and Paul to the meadow. They would announce the CD being released.

Why announce it? Everyone in the whole town knew it already.

Randy White slipped the knife into the sheaf behind the wide belt where it crossed the spine. He checked the mean little .25 automatic and snapped it into the holster in his boot. He dropped the heavy gold chain around his neck and put the big diamond earring in place.

Time to go to work. He got on the chopped hog and headed for the meadow. They would damned well not miss that little party today.

Annette picked up Paul, then Ralph. They were going to have a little private party to announce the CD, which had been named after the song that was surely going to take it to the top of the charts. *After the Blues Sit In.*

It was a little different than most of what the band did, but they got together and decided it was the kind of thing that could make them more than a ho-hum, yawn band. Gerry did have a voice that was good for this kind of thing.

Annette was the unofficial publicity agent for the band. She was going to be able to announce that the cover song had been played on a national network as a test. There were more than four thousand pre-sold copies. It was going to be big. She was sure it would hit the charts. She wouldn't be surprised for one second if it made the top hundred and not very surprised if it made top ten. The station that carried it was not one of the more popular ones.

The thing this would do is make the, as they called them, "Ho-hum crowd," well-known. Even a little minor fame in music.

Ralph deserved it. He would be totally lost with

fame, but he wrote what would be a huge hit. It was the kind of thing most bands in pop, country and pop-rock would want to do. The royalties from that would make Ralph come out top earner among them, though it would take a few royalty checks to make him know it. He would get royalties from several big names and hundreds of lesser names.

He had it in him to write a lot more hit music. It was a matter of him not looking for just the right word. It would come from him writing what he felt at the moment. That's what *After the Blues Sit In* was about.

Her mother had an old LP she played a lot. Janis Joplin. Ten other people had done *Me and Bobby McGhee* and had good sellers from it. It took her interpretation to make it a classic that would be around fifty or a hundred years later. She personally preferred Gordon Lightfoot's rendition, but that was why there was more than one song out there. Everyone liked a certain song that others didn't like or were neutral about. It was a matter of crossover appeal. This one had it in spades.

Life was like that. Ralph was the kind of person a lot of people would like in a lukewarm way. She thought he was the sexiest man in the world.

If she could just find a way to let him know that. He would *not* like a pushy woman.

"Well, I think this will be a special day for all of us!" she announced as Ralph put his guitar behind the rear seat.

Shirley Sanders looked in the mirror and smiled. Annette had told her the CD was going places. She was the backup vocals. She was going to be on the stage a lot for awhile.

Could she handle it? She wasn't that good ... well, maybe backup. It wasn't featured.

The big concern was performing in front of a lot of people. It was one thing when she was on the stage when there were fifty people in the audience. Could she hope to handle it if there were ten thousand? What if this went as far as Annette thought it would? Fifty thousand people?

She had to hide the fact she was so scared she would probably piss in her panties. Phyllis Jenkins had appeared at a concert where she did backup for Bob Seger. An emergency call. She said you have to get out there and pretend you're alone, practicing. The lights were so bright you couldn't see anything out front anyhow. Tune them out and pretend they're not there.

Maybe she could do that. Don't know til you've been there!

She went out to the car. Gerry, who had asked her to work with the band, seeing she was his special one, came. They headed for the meadow. Gerry asked if she thought the CD really would sell enough to where the band could get some new and better sound equipment. Annette was going to spring on the band that they were a hit before the CD was even released. It was going to be great fun!

Allen Norten grimaced at the mirror, sighed and said, “To hell with it!”

He didn’t want to be with that bunch of wannabes on the meadow. He was one hell of a lot better performer than all of them combined and knew it. He just couldn’t get a break! All he needed was that one little break where he would be noticed.

The mobs controlled music anymore. It was all to formula. He didn’t do things to their formula. He was the one who was innovative and original – which meant he was the one ignored.

The Angels were going to sell a few CDs with their latest copy. He had heard the song and it was nothing more nor less than a copy of Willie Nelson combined with Johnny Cash with just a little Bob Seger and Joe Cocker. Pure crap! All gravelly rasping voice.

He did a rock, then headed for the meadow. Time to be the sweet obsequious hanger-on.

Luke went by on his moto. Now, *there* was a man! He lived life the way he wanted it to be. He didn’t give a flying shit what the mob or anyone else wanted.

Luke was going to lay Ginger. He could see that if no one else did. The way she acted when she was around him made it obvious what she wanted. She wanted a *man*, and he was it!

Luke wouldn’t miss that opportunity. He wished he had a chance at a piece like that. If he could get in with her he would get his breaks. He could buy them.

Not gonna happen, Charlie!

Might as well head out. Maybe today wouldn’t be

too bad.

Phyllis Jenkins swore at the tangle her rings had made in her shawl. She cursed the things and tossed them onto the bed. A shawl would be out of place at the meadow anyhow. She just wanted to be better dressed than that bitch she pretended to think of as a friend.

Why did, every time she had a chance at something, something or somebody get between her and success?

She thought her one time backing Bob Seger would make it for her. She hadn't gotten one call.

Well, Seger didn't feature the backups like some. She didn't even make the local papers from that.

Her break would come. She just had to stay level and be the good friend of a lot of people she detested. She had to play the game a little better than they did.

She took a minute to hit a few tokes, then tore a few leaves from the basil plant on the windowsill to clean her breath. She rubbed a little in her hair. Marijuana always smelled in hair if you got close enough.

She was almost out. She took two hundred dollars from her stash of cash behind the drawer. She could score at the meadow.

She was as good as she was going to look now. Onward and upward!

Det. Rick Gordon dropped the file in the cabinet and grinned at Det. Glenda Kane, his sidekick in the violent crimes department. "That was a mean one. I hate when two people are so bitter at each other they neither one will tell the truth about anything. Too often it leads to one of them ending up dead."

"Yeah, and the survivor has hell for life from then until she dies," Glenda replied. "So busy blaming each other for everything they can't see it took two to tango. Sad and depressing."

"Well, today should be slow. A weekend a lot of people will stay home or go to the lake or meadow. We'll get to relax unless a leftover drunk from Saturday night causes a minor disturbance this department won't even hear about.

"You worked burglary with Fred yesterday?"

"Yeah. A couple of punks from Southend broke into MacDonald's. Nothing else."

"Think that CD the Angels made is going anywhere?"

"Oh, yeah! Annette told me it has already sold thousands before it's released..

"I'm not supposed to tell anyone yet, but you don't blab."

"They're a good bunch of kids. I hope they get some recognition. They've earned it."

They talked a bit about the happenings around town, then went to lunch. They got the call at three twelve that a body was found at the meadow.

"Emerald Meadow?" Glenda asked. "There are more than a hundred people there. What happened? A body was found? That sounds pretty sinister."

Rick asked a few questions as Glenda gathered their

satchels and cameras.

"Strangled. A girl Red Finch says may be Janet Fields.

"Glen, it was right at that little clump of scrub oak halfway to the middle on the east end. It was where a hundred people were running around. We're sure to have someone who saw something in that equation!"

"Yeah. Right!" She gave him the finger. He grinned.

And for Round Two...

Rick and Glenda spread out as soon as they had viewed the scene. They each had their method to get answers. This seemed like a strange event, no matter what. A woman was strangled in the middle of more than a hundred people. No one saw or heard anything.

He interviewed nine people who were closest to the scene. There were small tables in small areas with several people at each. Everyone walked around to talk with others they knew. No one could say with any certainty that any given person was at another table at a given time. Glenda was interviewing nine or ten on the other side.

Dr. Goldstein came to put the TOD at forty five to fifty minutes ago. Three to three ten, to give it a couple of minutes.

Rick went back to talk to Lena and Harry Marples. They were at the next table to the north. About fifteen feet away.

"We have a pretty definite time. Three o'clock to three ten," he said. "It would mean someone there only a few minutes before we were called. Less than an hour ago."

"Well, that handsome motorcycle bum was with her for a few minutes about then, I suppose," Lena said. "That singer with the CD they announced.

"They announced it at three. Annette. Ralph and the singer played it and sang it for us, so that was before then. Annette, Gerry and Ralph were right out there (pointing to a little knoll with a small gazebo on it. There was an amplifier and microphone in it), so they couldn't have been over here.

"I really didn't pay any attention to anything except the song. It really is good, don't you think?"

"It's selling before it's released, so would have to appeal to a lot of people," Rick agreed. "That means it was a distraction that allowed someone to kill a woman fifteen feet from you with little chance of being noticed.

"I was wondering how no one saw or heard anything. The killer used the show for distraction. No one on either side or between would see anything.

"Which motorcycle bum? There were two you could call that here.."

"Oh! The one they call Luke, I think. I hardly know the other one – and I don't want to. I don't want to know Luke, but he is always nice enough – well, so is that other one. They're just sort of scary, you know?"

"Randy has some kind of game he's playing. You get a feeling when he's around. You have to wonder where a biker bum got enough to have five thousand bucks worth of gold hanging around his neck."

"Ah!" Harry cried. "So those three places back there would be the only ones who could see it!

"You would think. That or someone passing by."

"Oh, nobody moved while they were doing the song

I don't think," Lena said.

"Except the killer," Harry added. Rick thanked them and went to the tables pointed out. No one was at the center one. The one on the right had Earl and Wilma Drier and their two small children. Wilma was over by the soda stand with the kids. Earl didn't pay any attention to the woman and her friends. She was a bit of a loose type of girl and several men had gone to talk with her. She seemed to hold the "Hello" kiss a little long and tight, which he didn't appreciate with his small children right there. He was a Johnny Cash fan most of his life and really got into the song. It was like he was at a concert fifteen years ago where Johnny had gone onto the stage to do *Big River*. If they remembered, several people were at the center table, then several others. They couldn't say who was there when the announcement was made – or if anyone was.

The other table had seen a few people go to Janet's table. She had faded into the background. They said she had people like that motorcycle guy and that scruffy one in the blue jean jacket, "On a day as hot as today." Four or five others had gone to her that they noticed in a way. They weren't all that kind. Some were the better class of people. They didn't pay much attention to that. They talked with some friends of their own when the announcement was made and Gerry and Ralph did the number. They hadn't looked at that table until Pat had sort of screamed for Red to call the police. There were some people there earlier, but they didn't really register. They were just some people at another table. They changed a lot, come to think of it. It was one of those where people would come to talk a few minutes, then drift away to other tables.

Rick thanked them and went to Glenda, who wasn't having any better luck.

"I went right to Randy White. He was there close to the gazebo, but he was talking to Emmy Stands, so he's out."

"He wasn't back by her table. I checked that, indirectly, but I didn't really have him in it."

"We'll have to trace her for the past few weeks to learn anything, I could bet," Glenda complained. "No one here can tell us anything – or will tell us. We have to dig it out."

There was a commotion down toward the far end of the meadow. Someone ran up to Dr. Goldstein to say something and he went at almost a run with the man. Rick raised an eyebrow at Glenda, who shrugged. They walked down that way. A teenage boy ran up to yell that there was another dead woman by the path to the creek.

They hurried to the gaggle of people and in to ask Doc what was going on.

"It seems we have quite a task," Goldstein answered. "A woman by the name of Phyllis Jenkins is dead. She was strangled very much like Fields was. Time of death within the last twenty minutes."

"Shit!" Glenda cried. Rick had to agree with that

assessment.

Two murders in the middle of more than a hundred people. The song was a distraction for the first and the investigation was the distraction for the second.

"Rick, I have a little something that may help you," Doc called. "There's an abrasion on the neck that tells me the killer wears a large ring with sharp corners on his left hand. He's powerful. There was a lot of crushing. The death was fast for this sort of thing."

"Thanks, Doc. It's something."

This one, they didn't have much to tell them who was close. Everyone was at the other end of the meadow, so it was possible someone was noted by someone else headed back there.

It was going to be a long investigation. It would be a matter of finding a connection between the two victims and someone else. It might be damned subtle. The victims were nineteen and twenty years old, which was an age where things might be a little harder to trace.

"Glen, see if anyone saw those two women together at anytime, even for ten seconds. I think the connection has to be here. Someone panicked for some reason and took one hell of a big chance."

Glenda nodded and circulated to ask where anyone saw either one other than the spot they were killed. It was vital to know if the two women were together at anytime.

They did get a break, maybe. Larry Hunter saw them talking near the gazebo where the song was performed about ten minutes before the announcement. Janis seemed upset or excited or something. He didn't really pay much attention to them.

"Think very carefully. Was anyone else very close to them?" Glenda asked.

"Well ... I think ... there was someone in the gazebo and someone standing there talking to him. That would be closest. People were passing by.

"I remember! They were bringing that amplifier there and hooking it up. There was that really rich guy with the Mercedes and one of those hippie types there. With the amp. I don't remember if it was exactly the same time or if they were where they saw the women. They might have heard them if Janet was talking loud. A word or two.

"They might have ... I don't know. Maybe they were already gone or maybe they came after. I wasn't concentrating on them, you know. They were just there and I saw them when I looked that way. I was there about four or five minutes. I was waiting for Helen. She came and we went on down to the table."

"The rich guy with the Mercedes? That would be Phillip Vincent?"

"You got me. I don't know anyone in that crowd, but he does run around with that whole bunch. He's the only one my age who does. They stay to themselves. I guess Ginger is among the really rich and we talk a lot. She's their age. Her Pop owns this whole end of the state."

"That's her horse over there?" Glenda pointed to

Gladiator. Larry said that was hers.

That was the only possible lead they found. Both Glenda and Rick thought it was more than fifty-fifty that meeting had something to do with their deaths.

"And I want a question answered that has me wondering for two years, but it can wait – unless there's a connection there. I've seen a certain person with another certain person ... two certain persons. Three."

"Rick?" Doc called. "I may have found something, but I don't have a clue as to whether it has any connection."

Rick and Glenda went over to him. "There is a definite odor of marijuana on her body. She tried to cover it with a spice. Maybe that Old Spice stuff. Basil. Users know it will hide pot odor for awhile.

"I know most of that age smoke a bit now and then, but they usually don't use it when they're going anywhere like this. I'll check her for cocaine and meth and such in the lab.

"I didn't detect anything like it with the other, so it might not have anything to do with anything."

"Thanks, Doc. It may have a connection with someone else. I don't think ... maybe it has a connection with this case, but it's iffy at best," Rick answered. "We'll have to stay around for awhile, but I doubt we're going to learn much more here."

They spent two more hours at the scene, but didn't learn much. They went back to the station to compare notes. Tomorrow was going to be spent checking out all the friends of the two dead women. Anything meaningful to the case would probably be found then.

"Glen, I want to check out something that came up. It's something that's may not have anything to do with this case, or it may. We won't know until we know what this case is about."

She agreed. "What is it?"

"Vincent. Do you know where he gets his money?"

"He's a stockbroker – I think. That's just what I've heard. I never asked."

"You would expect him to be around the Wells and that upper crust bunch. Why is he always around the sleaziest people?"

"Such as?"

"Nick Bianco, for one. We both know damned well that one's dealing in pot if nothing stronger. He doesn't wear long sleeves all the time in this heat because he's cold. I think he's hiding track marks."

"A couple told me he was setting up the gazebo with Vincent. I see what you mean. Jenkins had the smell of pot on her.

"Do you suppose Vincent's hooked on something? Bianco is his supplier?"

"That's one possibility. We have to keep that in mind when we talk to that group. Not direct. They wouldn't tell us if they know."

"You're the one who's good at that. I'll mostly be

thee to take notes or whatever. I'll have to talk to some of the females, but maybe you can give me a hint about what tō ask.

"I think I ... Harry said that about White and the gold chains. I wonder where he did get the money for that."

"It's more about what you pass over than what you ask. I've studied it. I can do it a little. Some people are naturals at it. People will spill their gut and not know they did.

"I checked White out all the way months ago. It's legitimate. He bought the stuff with money he got for an old Indian motorcycle he had restored to original.

"Should we start at the top? Ginger Wells?"

"Suits me."

They got the unmarked out and headed to the estate. Ginger seemed willing to tell them anything she knew, but she didn't know much.

"I was just there because some friends were and because I know all the band. Annette told me they were going to make a surprise announcement. It was about the CD going onto the charts almost before it was released.

"I got there early. I talked with everyone I knew for a few minutes. I don't remember when with who until the announce-ment. I was with Paul Stewart and Shirley Sanders when they did the song. Everything after is a jumble. Everybody was upset."

"How long before the announcement were you with them?"

"Maybe ten or fifteen minutes. That Norten bum was

trying to get me to talk to him and they more or less came to the rescue."

"Norten? Let's see," Rick checked his list. "Allen Norten? Sort of what we call scruffy?"

"Yeah. Like I was so thrilled because he wanted to.... I won't say, but you know what I'm saying."

"He was trying to get into your panties," Glenda said.

"Just the kind of date I dream about," she replied. "Him and Phyllis and Nick belong somewhere, but our group ain't it."

"Well, we need to know about a ten minute period. You and Stewart and Sanders would seem to be out of it.

"Do you know where any of the others were, definitely, at the time of the announcement? I mean, other than Gerry and Ralph and Annette."

"Not really. That motorcycle guy was talking to Gerry when Gerry went to the stage. I noticed him. He's sort of ... sexy, I'd guess you'd say. All the girls know where he was! That other motorcycle guy was talking with Phyllis, then with Phil, then they went to put the stuff on the stage. That was a few minutes before."

"The dangerous unsuitable magnet," Glenda said with a grin. "They always turn out to be a disappointment. At least to me. They're so stuck on themselves they don't have time or emotion for anyone else."

"I sort of got that idea. He does want to date me, but

we know what he's after. Paul says those little red dots on the fender of his bike are for the ones he's laid."

"Yeah. How many of them was twice?"

Ginger looked a bit shocked, then shrugged.

"I guess we'd better get on with this," Rick said. "Thanks."

Rick and Glenda went to the car. They would talk to Annette next. She had been on the stage and could have seen someone.

As they drove through town they saw Nick Bianco, so hailed him and asked if they could get a little information from him. He seemed very nervous. He said he didn't know anything, but they could ask.

"It's about yesterday. We have to know a few things about where people were and what they were doing for a few minutes. It's from when Annette went on the stage until the body was found.

"You and, let's see," he pretended to check his list. "A man called ... ah! Phil. You and Phil Vincent had set up the stage about half an hour before until ten minutes or so before. Allen Norten was talking to ... Phyllis Jenkins to one side. He was in the gazebo, she was outside the rail.

"Was anyone else around the stage at that time who you remember?"

"It wasn't Norten or Phyllis. It was Paul, Paul Binz, talking to Aimee Lang. She was with her parents and they wanted to meet him. He went with her."

"Hmm. Why would she say ... everybody has a

different story, but that was before ... so. Who else came by besides Fields."

"She just walked by and ... walked by. She wasn't with anyone. I called that Shirley was looking for her earlier. She said she already talked with her.

"I think she.... She said something to Phil when I went to the car for the microphones. She came there with, er, uh, with Phil and me. Randy was going away. I think he and Phil had some kind of deal or something one time and it went bad or something. "

"I see. That should have been explained yesterday, but it's probably not important. Let's see. The pot thing and the coke. That's not during the time ... I guess that's all. For now. I'll have some questions later about something else."

Nick was suddenly sweating and pale. He looked like he would faint. Rick had scored with that.

That was probably why he was so nervous. He had some stuff on him.

Maybe it would be best to let him go. See where and who he contacted.

"Uh, coke? What...? Pot? I don't, uh, oh, shit!"

"Phyllis got hers from you?" Glenda asked quickly. "She had used both before the meadow."

"Jeez! I ain't, I mean, I have to, uh, that is.... Oh, shit!"

"You're pretty obvious. We aren't on narco section now, but you're way out on overtime for a bust. You're hooked on snow?" Rick asked.

"You don't know how I've tried to kick it! I can't!

Oh, shit!"

"Don't deal anymore and you might get by," Rick counseled. "When your clients start getting murdered things are going to come out."

"He'll cut me off. I can't.... Oh, shit!"

"Just tell them you're getting hot because of the deaths," Glenda said. "You're being watched a lot closer now. You can't move without us knowing."

"Yeah. Maybe ... I can't think. I'm scared!"

"Work it out," Rick suggested. He and Glenda got in the car and drove off. Glenda radioed in to have a twenty-four-seven surveillance on Nick Bianco.

"I think we just won a minor victory," Glenda said. "Maybe we can find out who his supplier is."

They pulled up in front of Annette's apartment. Gerry and Ralph were there. That would be alright. They were the three who couldn't have killed anyone at that time.

They didn't see anything from the stage. They were facing about thirty degrees to the right of that table.

"That Luke character was over there when I went on the stage. Not at that table, but on that side," Annette said. "He was talking to Ginger Wells. She was laughing at something.

"I remember that because he's the type who you would call handsome and built and dangerous. You know right away that he's nothing but trouble if you tumble to him. He would use you and throw you out before you knew what hit you.

"You look and wonder, but he's a definite no-no.

Him and Randy. Randy may be okay."

The others hadn't noticed anything.

"Did any of you notice Bianco around after he set up the stage?" Glenda asked. They looked at each other and said they hadn't noticed him He was probably with Phil and that Norten bum who thought he was god's gift, but he wasn't even a consolation prize.

"That was ... I passed them when I went to the gazebo. Maybe six or eight minutes before I made the announcement."

They chatted a bit, thanked the three and left.

"Norten has come up one time too many!" Rick insisted. "Him next."

They checked the addresses and headed out Elm to Oak Circle. A big shiny Mercedes was sitting out front of Norten's house. Bianco was at the door.

"Our little victory has gotten a little bigger," Rick said. "Now our Mr. Vincent has some serious questions to answer."

They had stopped just before turning into the circle. Norten's house was second on the left.

Rick quickly backed up to where the car couldn't be seen from that house and he and Glenda went to watch from behind a large yew on the corner.

Vincent had come to the door. Bianco said something that involved arm waving and such. Vincent handed him something and he went to the car. Vincent must have given him the keys. He opened the passenger door and leaned inside for a few seconds, then backed out with a package, locked the car and went to the house. He was looking around like a cornered rabbit.

"I think we've found our supplier to the local street dealers," Rick said. "That must be the kind of stock he brokers."

"And Janet rode to the meadow with them. That package was in the car. Phyllis was a user.

"You know what I think?"

"That's not hard to figure. One of them."

"It wasn't Nick. It wasn't Vincent."

"Which leaves us with good old scruffy Norten!"

"Or White? The other biker? The one who nobody mentions much? The one who's always in the background somewhere?"

Rick nodded and looked grim.

Proving It

Glenda called in for a squad from narco to come to that house and make a sudden raid. The squad was on alert since before they started for Norten's. Rick had a feeling that drugs and drug dealers were behind some part of it, if not all of it. Three minutes.

Glenda was ready to get out of the car as soon as the squad screeched to a half in front of the house. Rick said he wanted to find Luke and Randy. He wanted to be there when they learned about the raid. They would be at Prince's Pool Parlor this time of day on a Sunday.

She thought, then nodded. They headed for the pool hall. Randy's bike was out front Glenda said Luke would be at Diamond Diner, ten to one. Rick got out. Glenda went to the driver's seat and waved.

Rick went inside. Randy was talking on his cellular. He seemed upset.

Rick waited until he rang off to say, "Bad news?"

"You don't know! Two years of work may have just gone down the drain!"

"Because of a drug raid?"

"Yeah. Bad timing."

"Norten killed those girls."

"I think so."

"It will expose Vincent as the main supplier in

town?"

"In a lot more than town. A hell of a lot more."

"You're federal."

"Yeah. Don't blow my cover."

"What do you need? I'll try to help."

White thought for a minute. "How good are you at acting?"

"Acting?"

"Like in those stupid karate and violence flicks."

"Never tried. I know some judo, but not much."

"Could you use a move or two to disarm me and arrest me?"

"We could try."

"I'll jump up and reach for the knife in my belt in back. You can do an arm twist, I'll drop the knife, then you give the back of my neck a chop. I'll drop and you cover me before I can reach the knife. Cuff me and call for a car.

"Maybe I'll have a lawyer who can get Vincent off while leaving Norten and Bianco swinging in the wind."

"Worth a try!"

White suddenly jumped up, turning the table over. Rick jumped up to the side and grabbed the arm bringing the knife around to twist upward and back. White yelled, yanked the arm away and lunged at Rick, who did a realistic judo chop to the back of the neck. White dropped, then tried to get to the knife. Rick had his Glock out and pointed right between his eyes. He froze and slowly put his hands up. Rick cuffed him and jerked him to his feet in what looked like an unnecessarily rough way. He shoved him as roughly toward the door.

There were seven or eight other customers in the place who heard Rick saying, "You have the right to an attorney. If you cannot afford one...." as he marched him out front. He radioed for a cage car. Glenda came screeching up.

"Situation under control," Rick said.

Four of the customers were in the door, gawking.

"He's a nutcase! I was asking him about the meadow. I said something about Norten and he was all of a sudden jumping around like a madman!

"I think he's on something! He's got a lot of explaining to do, for sure!"

Glenda caught on. She was anything but slow.

"Really? I just got a com that Norten and three others were busted in a raid at Norten's place. Drugs. A hundred pound bale of pot and more than three kilos of coke, not to mention a brick of snow and gallons of crack rocks."

That would be real. "So. Got anything to say, crud?"

"My lawyer will say anything that needs saying."

The cage car came and Rick shoved him in. He said he'd meet them at the station.

On the way he told Glenda about White being a federal agent who was building a case against Vincent. He would set it up so that Norten and Bianco would go down, but Vincent and White would walk.

"Won't Norten give us Vincent?"

"I don't know how they'll set that up."

"Your honor, we will prove, beyond doubt, that the incident was manufactured by the prosecution, that what was said by them is false.

"It is possible that there was some misunderstanding, but the excessive and totally unnecessary violence displayed by that cop is inexcusable."

White called him to whisper in his ear. He stood and continued, "My client says he feels the officer misunderstood him, as well. That both of them may be at fault. That nothing will be accomplished here, other than a lot of bad feeling where none are necessary. So he lost a fight in a pool hall. It's not the first time.

"If I may make a short statement, then meet with the prosecution in a sidebar? We can perhaps dispense with a lot of time-consuming testimony."

The judge nodded.

"My client was in a pool hall restaurant when the officer came in to speak with him about the recent murders at Emerald Meadow. They were discussing who could have killed those women. The officer made a statement, I hope he'll confirm, that my client was observed speaking with one victim, a Miss Phyllis Jenkins, just moments before the discovery of her body."

He looked at Rick, who looked thoughtful, then agreed that was what happened.

"What my client explained was that he was incensed at the accusation he felt was implied. He jumped up and said that, should he kill anyone, it would not be by strangulation. He reached for the knife he carries, merely to show the officer that he would use such an implement.

"He feels the misunderstanding was there. He was not attacking the officer, but realizes it may have looked that way.

"I can well imagine that the officer felt he was under attack. He reacted as any of us would, if a bit excessively.

"May we approach the bench?"

"Approach. The officer also."

The judge put his hand over the microphone. "Officer Gordon, do you agree with this story? Is it *probable*, not just vaguely *possible*, the events occurred in the described manner?"

Rick thought, then slowly nodded. "I did over-react. White was not threatening until that moment. He did say something about using ... *this* ... and reached behind him. I simply reacted in the manner of my training. He didn't actually say he was going to use it on me. I may, I guess you would say, 'probably,' have misunderstood."

"Thank you. You may return to your places."

They went to the tables and sat. The judge had the reporter read a couple of things from the lawyer's statement, then checked against the prosecution's opening statement.

"Case dismissed. Court is adjourned."

They went back to the station. They wouldn't have

to appear at the trials of Norten and Bianco. The records stated that the squad was called by Glenda because of the report of an undercover operative who had been watching the house.

Rick was greatly surprised that a state operative was actually watching Norten and Bianco. Randy knew about it and had the operative make a report, sealed, that was what happened. Glenda filed testimony in an affidavit that wasn't questioned.

"Glen? How did Vincent manage to get his case filed separately?"

"The way I understand it, he was a total innocent. He knew Bianco had left a package in his car, but had no idea it was a brick of heroin! He knew Norten was addicted to heroin. He was trying to help him get into withdrawal therapy. A doctor at the state facility produced a form where Vincent had filed for therapy for a friend who was unnamed."

"And?"

"Both Norten and Bianco refused to implicate him."

Rick called White. "How did you get them not to tie Vincent's ass around a lamp post?"

Randy laughed. "A drug producer makes a little threat about what could happen if they do?"

"Why was that enough to get his case separated? Won't they be called? Who was the third person there at the raid?"

"A deal with a judge to stop the loss of cover for a big-shit federal agent. The third person was a girl-friend who was asleep in the bedroom. She probably didn't have a clue. Either that or she's a hell of a lot better actress than her IQ would seem to allow."

"Dumb as a stump?"

"And borderline retarded. It's the best Norten could do."

They chatted a few minutes. Nothing else was new. Rick's case would be resolved with the conviction of Norten for murder. Be glad. It was dangerous as all hell to be up against those people.

The following day the court bailiff called. Rick and Glenda were to be called in the case.

"We are? Why?" Rick asked.

"Something about one of them hinting that he killed two women at Emerald Meadow."

Rick got another call not two minutes later.

"It's going to hit the fan. My cover's going out the window. We'll lose the way to close down a route from Peru to Mexico, then to the states. Fuck! Two years and I was almost there!

"You know damned well that he'll rat out Vincent to try for a deal."

"Maybe we can find a way to use the fact that he's an addict to make his testimony in that area worthless?"

"How?"

"Maybe ... I don't know."

"Well, You're due at nine. They'll probably put you on fast. I'm through before noon, in all probability."

They talked about finding a way to keep Vincent's name from coming up. They would have to wait to see what was said and done before Rick testified. Glenda would probably not be called, but had to be there in case her testimony was needed.

"Randy? Whose name can I drop? Someone at least suspected who's higher than Vincent?"

"I can't ... Samosa and Guerra are two names we're keeping a close on."

"I may have an idea. Be ready to watch and listen to everything Vincent does after I drop a bomb."

Damning Testimony

"Officer Gordon, you are here because Mr. Norten made a reference in this court that may prove a connection with the murders of two women at the Emerald Meadows Recreation Area.

"Is Mr. Norten a suspect in those murders?"

"Among others, yes."

"And what connection would keep you, considering your investigation, from charging him with those crimes? Is the evidence too thin?"

"I don't understand the question."

"Mr. Norten has as much as admitted to those murders in this court. It is why you are here. Why didn't you file charges the moment you learned of that? Is it because there is someone else, someone more powerful, above him?"

"*Ob*jection! Is the prosecutor questioning the witness or testifying in his stead?"

"Sustained."

"I will rephrase. Are you suspicious that Mr. Norten may have committed those murders at the order of someone else?"

White, who was in the audience, rolled his eyes. The prosecutor knew who that was supposed to be.

"Yes." That got a shocked look from White.

"Who is that person?"

“We can’t be sure at this point. Several names were mentioned.”

“And is that person in this community?”

“I said several. One may be.”

“Who, Officer Gordon. Who is suspected?”

“Until I have some proof, I won’t give a single name. There is a Mr. V., then a paid murder by a man named Guerra....”

Glenda had a sudden coughing fit. The judge rapped his gavel. Norten slid down in his seat and looked totally lost.

“A Sr. Samosa, but that’s also a pai....”

Glenda had another coughing fit. She stood, coughed again and pointed to the door. She went out. Norten was gasping, pure terror on his face.

“No!” Norten screamed. Bianco, also at the defense table, was as terrified.

“Oh, my god! We’re both dead!” Norten sobbed. “I killed them. No one else had anything to do with it. Phyllis bought some stuff from me and Janet saw it and she was going to burn me and I didn’t know what to do and I killed Janet, then Phyllis said she really had me by the balls and I was going to supply her with enough so she could make a little on the side or I was gone for the big count and, oh, my god!”

“Why the reaction to those names?” Rick asked. The judge rapped the gavel.

“Because they’re big in the ... because they ... I refuse to say anything else!” Bianco cried.

“Are you admitting to the drug charges with this?”

the judge asked.

"Yes," From Bianco.

"And you, Mr. Norten?"

"Yes. I admit it all. I killed them and I was dealing and whatever else. I can't kick my habit. I may as well be dead. I killed Florence Malden two months ago in Eastonville. It don't matter no more."

"Your Honor, Judge, we know a lot that Vih ... a certain person doesn't know we know," Bianco said. "We can't stay alive long, no matter what. I swear we won't ever say anything else about anybody we might know about if they leave us alone. If they leave us alone. The DEASS get nothing from us if they leave us alone."

Vincent, sitting in back, got up and went out. White smirked and gave a thumbs up to Rick when everyone was looking at Bianco.

"The DEASS?" a defense lawyer asked.

"DEA Stupid Shitheads."

"Court is in recess until two o'clock. Witness is excused," the judge said. He went out the door behind the chair. A man in a blue stiff suit went toward the defense table from the audience. Rick tensed. Randy gave a slight nod. He would be a government man, not a silencer.

He found Glenda in front and said it had worked fifty times as well as they'd hoped. They headed for the station.

"So. I guess we're now caught in an international drug case?" Glenda accused.

"It would seem. If we can't get out of it."

They went to lunch. When they got back to the station Randy was sitting there.

"Well, seems you helped my case along a good bit! It may be enough. Vincent can't get around what Bianco and Norten are spilling. They got some papers from Vincent's car a few times, copied them and put them back. It seems your Mr. Vincent is careless about what he leaves in that car. Bianco also has a couple of photos he took when Vincent was meeting with three people, two of whom you mentioned in court. They're dated by the camera. It wasn't known they were in the US at those times. They won't testify in court. That would be suicide, and a very messy suicide.

"The third is a man called El Leon, which means 'The Lion' – from Argentina, with offices in Peru. A transshipping firm. His real name is Hans Gangermann. I think he'll be the link we have to break. He's running the stuff all the way.

"You can tag Vincent with what you have?"

"No," Glenda replied. "For drugs, slam dunk. For the murders, no. Norten's story is too logical. It may be what went down, but none of us think so."

They chatted until it was time to go back to the court. That was short. Judge Vernon called the court into session and announced that, without objection, he would pass sentence for the drug parts of the case. It would be to another trial to determine the murder sentence, though that was admitted, so could be handled as a prosecuted case, without objection.

Rick stood and said he objected to the murder case being completed unless testimony for official use could be taken as affidavit to be included in the records.

"Defense? Concluded after affidavit?" Vernon asked.

"No objection."

"Due to the quantity of drugs confiscated I am guidelined to pass a sentence of no less than five years. I may, after consideration, add to that as I see fit. As murder is involved, it is a consideration.

"The murder will be tried in separate court, thus I consider that the defendants have cooperated in most ways. I pass sentence of five years with reservation that future acts or discoveries may be used to add to that sentence.

"So ordered. Court adjourned."

The bailiff delivered the notice that the trial for murder session would be the next day at 9:00AM and would be held in recess at that time until affidavit could be rendered as to agreement with the state court system, such affidavit to be garnered at the police station.

Everyone went back to the job or home.

In the morning Rick met Glenda at the restaurant where they had breakfast at times. They both got a call at the same time.

Norten had Oded in his cell. He was dead.

"Which will let Vincent off for that," Glenda complained. “We both know he didn’t suicide.”

“He might have. I think he did. No one could get in there to inject him. Now no one can testify that Vincent ... maybe they can!

“Let’s go over to holding and have a little talk with Bianco.”

“He’s being held in section two. Norten was in section one. There’s no way Bianco could have killed him.”

“No. I know that. I have another idea. Call Randy and have him in the recording room at interrogation ‘C’ in twenty minutes.”

She looked a question, then nodded. “He’s running scared. He can’t know that it was suicide unless Norten told him he was going to end himself?”

“Uh-huh.”

Rick made a requisition form for Bianco. Norten was dead. He had to have some questions answered while everything was fresh. Billy Crews, warden, said, “Before he finds out it really was suicide? That there was a note?”

“Oh, yeah! There was a note?”

“We would never call it suicide if there wasn’t a note. With the evidence we would have to call it under suspicious circumstances, but he was watched twenty four seven. No one else was within fifteen feet of that cell after dinner. The stuff was gotten to him before that, somehow.”

Rick laughed. Billy asked what was so funny.

“He delivered the stuff. They have dinner in their

cells. There was a little something extra on his tray.

"Who delivered the tray?"

"Irma Silas. She brings the stuff from her restaurant on contract. We know she can be bribed to take the inmates cigarettes and more."

Rick nodded and went to take Bianco to the interrogation room. He had coffee delivered, then sat to look at Bianco for a minute, then to shake his head.

"What's the deal? Why bring me here?"

"To try to save your ass," Rick replied. "You heard about Norten?"

"Norten? What? I haven't heard anything."

"He's dead. Supposed suicide. OD."

"In here? He got the stuff to OD in here?"

"Uh-huh. He knew too much. You do, too. He has to shut you up or the bigger ones will shut him up. They have to break the link. All he'll really get out of it is a short reprieve. No one's going to be left around to say anything about anyone."

Bianco shrunk down a bit "No one can stop them. They can get me in here and in state a lot easier."

"Give us Vincent. It can be by affidavit and you won't be where they can find you easily. I can arrange ... do you speak Italian?"

"Yeah. That's all Mom and Pop spoke around the house. Their English sucked."

"So you could blend fast in, say, Rome?"

"I was there once. Yeah. Trouble is, I talk and never get there."

"Like Norten talked?"

He thought. "I don't have a chance."

"One. What do you have? Beside the pictures and the copies we have? We know damned well that's not all."

"You have the pics and sheets?"

"Norten had a note in the bunk in case anything like what happened happened."

He thought a bit more, then asked for a piece of paper and a pencil with sign language. He wrote a few things on the paper and handed it to Rick. He pointed to the recorder on the table.

"I'll have to take my chances. There could be a reason they'll leave me alone for awhile. I can show them I can keep clammed."

"Your call." He turned off the recorder.

"When do I go?"

"Now. You left your cell, which they could have bugged, and came here and disappeared. We have about half an hour before they'll even ask questions. It should take that long to interview you.

"Agent? We agreed to get him to Rome, then he's on his own."

There were two raps on the mirror. Rick took Bianco to the door and they went out through the service hall. An old thinner man and a stocky slightly younger man, both of whom looked Mexican, went out the maintenance room door to the parking lot and got in a rattletrap old Plymouth to drive away. Rick waited half an hour and went out the front. Glenda was there.

"How'd it go?"

“Right down the line as planned. Whoever’s watching ... no one. They couldn’t get back there to watch. They’ll have some kind of bug in the cell. Maybe just outside the vent.”

Rick got the binoculars from the glove case of the unmarked and went around back to study the wall around the vent to that cell. He found a very small pickup glued just below the sill outside. He smirked and went in and to the cell, where he made a few noises, then swore in a low voice, then made sounds like he was laying on the bunk for a minute, then went silently out.

“They’ll wait for him to wake up. Nervous time will come in about two hours is my guess. He’ll be on a plane they can’t trace,” he told Glenda in the car. “He’s Rome’s problem now. I doubt he’ll survive long there, but you never know. Maybe he’s learned where that kind of life leads.”

“Yeah. One in three hundred do learn.”

They waited at the station until Randy came in. They then headed for the Central National Bank 12 miles away at Pleasantdale and to the safe deposit boxes. Number four twenty two, combination 14L 12R 26L 3R. That opened the outer door, then Randy took the key Bianco said was under the third begonia on the right from the door on his porch to open the inner door. He slid the box out, rifled through a few of the papers, then took out an envelope with a sheet of paper and ten or so pictures. He looked at the top picture and whistled.

"Herr Gangermann, you're going down for the count if you're ever anywhere we can extradite you."

There were four pictures of airports in Colombia, Nicaragua, Mexico and Texas. All featured a plane with Canadian numbers. Two had Gangermann at the port. One had Vincent. They were not looking at the camera. They didn't know their pictures were being taken.

Randy looked on the back of the sheet, but there wasn't anything on it.

He checked the backs of the pictures. One had a schedule on it. It was the one from Texas. There were dates. Every fifteen days. The next was due in six days.

"I think perhaps we'll have a nice little surprise waiting for that one," Randy said. "What are these little stars for? I have to know that. There's one by the next date."

There were only two of the stars for this year. They didn't have a hint.

Rick took the picture and studied the schedule, then turned it over. The date was at the end of last year. Gangermann was in that picture.

"You know what I think maybe?" Rick asked.

"You think Gangermann will be on that flight," Glenda replied. "That is far too much to ask of life!"

Randy packed everything back and took the envelope to put under his loose shirt. They relocked the box and left. Vincent's trial would be in nine days. That might work out very well!

The sleek jet taxied down the runway and to the private hangar. There were twelve DEA agents waiting when the electric doors opened and the plane stopped outside. There was a van truck inside with four men when the agents went in. Those four were in a government holding cell in the nearby terminal. The team looked like four workers and two hangar managers. The rest were hidden.

They pulled the plane in with the little puller-dozer and closed the doors. The port opened and the pilot came down the ramp to ask where George and Harry were. The agent said in the hospital with botulism poisoning.

A distinguished man in a suit came to demand someone get his suitcases and Matilda's and deliver them to the Royal Hotel, penthouse suite.

A blond bimbo sexpot came to pout in Spanish that she always had trouble with her hair when she flew.

They came down the steps where they were met by two agents with a warrant to search the plane. Gangermann was indignant and was going to have the government and the airport and the population for miles around on their knees! This was outrageous! He came there three times a year for more than six years! He was beyond reproach! He wanted his lawyer there before they stepped one foot onto his property! He would sue the US for fifty billion dollars!

"Yes, Sir. Noted. You may go to your hotel where you may call all the lawyers your want. Call your congressman, too, except that a congressman from Argentina won't fare too well in Texas."

The team opened the lower cargo bin. "Jesus Holy Christ!" an agent exclaimed. "There has to be half a ton of processed cocaine in here!"

"Que?" the bimbo asked.

Gangermann bolted for the door. There was an agent with an AK-47 there. He came back.

"Let's see your identification," an agent said to the bimbo.

"Que?"

"Su passaporte, por favor."

"Yo no hay! Hans dice no es necesario aqui con el!" (I don't have one! Hans said I don't need one here if I am with him!"

"Sam! There's about twenty bales of pot in the rear baggage hold!" an agent called.

"Mr. Gangermann, I think it's going to be a long time before you get back to Argentina – if you ever do. You have the right to remain silent. Anything you say may be held in evidence against you. You have...."

Randy read the transcripts and handed them to Rick and Glenda. Gangermann refused to say anything. He had a team of ten lawyers, the top lawyers in the state. Everything owned by him in the states was confiscated. His accounts were frozen.

"Hmm. He has more than a hundred million in cash in two banks here. We used an hour's interest on it to send Matilda Remedio home first class. She was too dense to know what was going on. To her, she found a sugar daddy who would take her all over the world.

"Nobody says 'Sugar daddy' anymore. My parents always did.

"We showed Vincent the picture of him on Gangermann's plane. He almost passed out. I think we can break him down pretty fast. If we don't get him for ordering the murders he's going away for life plus, no matter what."

"What was the street value of that load?" Glenda asked. "Not the overdone hype. Actual."

"Something over ... where ... here it is. Seventy two million, which will be twenty percent over, so fifty five million or so."

"What would anyone do with that kind of money?" Rick asked. "It's downright obscene."

"I could use about a hundred grand. That would be plenty for what I want," Glenda said. "I could never be a rich bitch who laid around and didn't do anything. Against my nature."

"Give me enough to pay off the mortgage and pay the taxes for ten years. I can get by with what I make very nicely without that hanging over my head," Rick said. "I couldn't be a bum. I'd get fat and die of boredom in a year."

"Well, Vincent's trial is in two days. Have a nice

weekend. See you in court," Randy replied. He waved and went out.

"What will Gangermann get?" Glenda asked. "If he wasn't richer than Midas I'd say no question, ten life sentences."

"He's too rich. Maybe two life sentences, concurrent. He'll serve twenty five years before he's eligible for parole. He'll live like a king while he serves. That country club in Florida, probably. Golf course, tennis, two Olympic pools, catered meals and whatever else he can pay for. He'll have them send a couple million from Argentina to tide him over."

"Sheee!"

They straightened up the files, got what they would need for the trial together, studied it to be sure they hadn't left anything out and went home.

"We will show that Phillip Vincent did distribute drugs in this state, minimum. We will show that this involvement led to two murders.

"Yes, the murders were committed by another. That person died under suspicious circumstances while incarcerated for dealing the drugs Phillip Vincent imported on the streets. This we will prove.

"Phillip Vincent is in an impossible trap of his own design. We will show that he has laundered tremendous sums of money gotten from the sale of drugs. He will tell you he is a licensed broker, and that is true. That does not explain exactly *what* he was brokering.

"We will show that Phillip Vincent did conspire and consort with a major drug producer in Argentina to import those drugs into this country. That investigation had led to charges of corruption of two major officers in the airport security field as well as charges of extreme quantities of illegal drugs being brought here.

"There are many other charges against Phillip Vincent. They will be explored during this trial.

"Thank you."

Peter Vanderhaven, the prosecutor, took his seat.

"Defense? Do you wish to make an opening statement?" Judge Vernon asked.

The lawyer on Vincent's left (he had three) stood. "Only to ask why those two cops are here, your honor?" He pointed to Glenda and Rick, sitting at the prosecutor's table.

Vernon sighed. They had been through this in motions. "Asked and answered, but I will allow prosecution to make this one last explanation. Prosecutor?"

"Because they conducted a murder investigation that uncovered the deeds of the defendant."

"But why are they sitting...?"

"You, Sir, are two words from a contempt citation! You will conduct yourself in a manner that indicates you have some small knowledge of courtroom procedures!

"Prosecutor? Call your first witness. Both prosecution and defense will ask their questions at the proper time. You will treat the witnesses and each other with respect. I hope that is quite clear!"

"Call Lucas Hopkins."

That took Rick by surprise. He knew Hopkins was on the witness lists, but thought it was just because he had been at the meadows. He didn't see why he was being called in a drug investigation.

Hopkins took the stand.

"Mr. Hopkins, what is your occupation?"

"I'm a private investigator."

"And what is your connection with this case?"

"Accidental. I was investigating a person's past for

the father of another person at the party. Several people at that party, to be honest about it. The one in question came about because of the major subject. I was investigating Phillip Vincent because of business dealings. The other was often seen with Phillip Vincent."

"And what did you learn about this person?"

"Vincent? That he was associating with numerous street drug dealers."

"I meant the one who is dead."

"That he was a heroin junkie and dealer in marijuana and cocaine."

"What was the name of that dealer?"

"Allen Frederick Norten."

"How did he die?"

"He is supposed to have committed suicide by overdose of heroin while incarcerated."

"You don't believe that to be true?"

"I have reservations. How did he get the drug into his cell to use to kill himself?"

"You believe Phillip Vincent is involved in that?"

"Personally, let's say I find it not to be beyond him."

"And you say this because?"

"Because I heard him speaking on his cellular telephone. He said that two people had to be silenced before the whole group were in hot water."

"When was this?"

"While the stage was being set up at the party. Perhaps half an hour before the first body was discovered."

"You don't believe he was speaking about the women who were murdered there?"

"I did at the time. Later, when it was discovered that Norten killed the women, it occurred to me that Norten was twenty feet away. He wasn't talking on a phone. That had to be about somebody else. Other statements indicated that it was not women to whom he referred."

"Thank you." He looked at the defense table. "Your witness."

"What made you jump to the conclusion that he was speaking about this Norten person?" Orson Oscar Oliver, a defense attorney demanded.

"I didn't. Later, when the narco squad arrested Norten, something else said on that call came to mind.

"There was a brick of heroin in the console of Mr. Vincent's car that led to the arrests. Mr. Vincent had said the main person to be hit was a user and had the nerve to put some stuff in his car. The second was a person who was always with that person and was suspicious. He may be an undercover narc, but that didn't really seem likely. He should be shut up, just to be sure."

Oliver didn't seem to know what else to ask, so he sat.

"What was the distance between you and Mr. Vincent when the alleged call was made?" Thurston Thomas Tilton, another defense attorney asked from his seat.

"Maybe fifteen feet. Twelve to fifteen feet."

"Oh? You overheard that conversation clearly at fifteen feet?"

"Yes. It's less than half the distance from you to me right now. I hear you clearly at twice that distance."

"There is not a lot of background noise here. No further questions."

"Redirect!" Vanderhaven cried. "Mr. Hopkins, what was the situation as to background noise at that place and time?"

"There was very little. The party was quite a distance from that point. They were mostly on the center of the meadow, not up at the end where the gazebo is located. There were a few people at the tables, perhaps forty to fifty feet away."

"Thank you."

"Still, there was background noise. Nothing further."

"Not anymore than here. I am a trained listener."

"Your honor!" Tilton yelled. "There was no question asked!"

"No, you made a comment in improper form. Mr. Hopkins merely forbade you to impeach him by innuendo.

"Thank you, witness. You may step down."

"Call Harold Wells."

Another unexpected. What was he even doing there? – Oh! Luke was investigating for a father.

"Mr. Wells, you are well-known in this community. You, in fact, own and maintain Emerald Meadow as a gift to this town.

"What is your connection to this case?"

"I am the person who employed Mr. Hopkins."

"And what was the nature of that employment?"

"Mr. Vincent approached me twice with business propositions. I was suspicious of the way those propositions were worded. Mr. Hopkins was already in my employ to determine if persons who were supposedly attracted to my daughter were actually attracted to her or only to the fact that we are wealthy."

"Well, I've spoken with your daughter and she said she was attracted to Mr. Hopkins."

"Mr. Vanderhaven, we seem prudes to our daughter. We are not. I also checked on Mr. Hopkins most carefully. He is known for pursuing a dalliance when it is offered, in some cases. The ones he was investigating were thought to be after her for money. He is not that type. By comparison, he is far more acceptable. My wife and I pretended we thought Mr. Hopkins was a motorcycle bum and unacceptable. That made him attractive to her, but she was raised with a system of values. I believe she would not pursue such a relationship far."

Judge Vernon rapped his gavel. "Questions and answers, Mr. Vanderhaven? Not just answers."

"Sorry, your honor. I wished to establish the pragmatism of Mr. Wells.

"Sir, what did Mr. Hopkins report concerning Mr. Vincent?"

"Hearsay!" Tilton yelled.

"Mr. Tilton, it is not necessary to scream. I can hear

as well as Mr. Hopkins.

"Mr. Wells, do you have this information in writing?"

"Yes. Of course."

"Then you may read it to answer questions. Proceed."

Mrs Wells brought a thick file to hand to the bailiff, who took it to Wells. Wells quickly went through to take out a smaller file. "Vincent" was on the label tab. He sat and looked expectant.

"Your honor! This will take forever!"

"You're the one who objected. Live with it. Ask your questions, Mr. Vanderhaven."

"What was the report on Mr. Vincent?"

"Let's see. I find it very suspicious that V. meets so often with several people. They are typical of druggies and street dealers anywhere..

"Next, Norten is a dealer, as suspected. He tried to sell me pot. He didn't have on his jacket. There are track marks on his arms. Bonati ditto, minus the tracks.

"Hmm. Next. V. asked me if I smoked. I said not often. He suggested in a roundabout way that I could make a lot of money selling pot.

"Next. V. said he knows a wholesale deal on crack. I said I would never have anything to do with crack or crackheads.

"I would strongly advise against any business dealings with V. Norten was stoned and said he had to get a new lot. He went directly to V. and came back with twenty two-ounce bags. I said that was a dealer quantity. He said of course it was. It was wholesale.

"He said V. was too often with...."

"If you will pause for a moment here? Read that last part very clearly, please?"

"Right! 'I would strongly advise against dealings with V. Norten was stoned and said he had to get a new lot. He went directly to V. and came back with twenty two-ounce bags. I said that was dealer quantity. He said of course it was. It was wholesale.' That part?"

"Yes. Thank you.

"If your honor will allow? We can save some time here if Mr. Hopkins will stand and answer one question?"

"You are still under oath, Mr. Hopkins. Proceed."

"Is that a true reading of what you discovered and reported?"

"Yes."

"About a V!" Tilton yelled. "That could mean anyone!"

"The file is labeled. It is labeled 'Vincent.' The capital V in all cases in that documentation is Mr. Phillip Vincent," Hopkins answered.

"Not asked, but a clarification. I'll allow it," Judge Vernon said. "Proceed, Mr. Vanderhaven."

"Nothing further at this time. Reserve recall."

"Defense?"

They conferred for a few seconds. "No questions at this time."

"Call Officer Gordon."

Rick took the stand.

"Officer, you handled the murder investigation concerning the two women, Miss Fields and Miss Jenkins?"

"I did."

"You have reported that the raid on the Norten house was due to an anonymous agent of the department?"

"Officer Kane did, yes."

"Was that agent Mr. Hopkins?"

Rick looked at Hopkins, who slightly nodded.

"No comment. Identifying the agent here would make him or her useless in further investigations."

Hopkins grinned and gave a thumb up.

"Then how can you use that information here? For the clarification of the defense counsel?"

"Sworn affidavit before Judge Vernon or other judge."

"Agreed," Vernon said.

"Very well. You were investigating Mr. Vincent for the murders at Emerald Meadow. The drug investigation was a tangental case?"

"Yes. We turned that part of it over to narcotics, who contacted the federal government due to the quantities under investigation. The charges are to be transferred to federal court after resolvement here on local and state charges."

"The connection with South American producers and distributors came about because of your connections discovered?"

"So I am informed. It isn't within my province. It was reported to this department because we initiated investigation." Rick didn't know what he was doing. This seemed farfetched to his interests.

"In what way was Mr. Vincent involved in your investigations?"

"Solely in that the dead man who admitted to the killings made a suggestive statement that he had to kill them or his supply would be cut off and he would probably be hit."

"Hit?"

"Expression. Killed by a hired killer."

"Of which, in a sense, Mr. Norten admitted to?"

"Yes."

"And Mr. Norten alluded to the one who would cut off his supply as being Mr. Phillip Vincent?"

"Mr. Vincent was his accused supplier. The connection is obvious."

"Yes, it is. Thank you. I believe we have established motive for murder, if not drug dealings, directly.

"Your witness, defense."

Tilton stood this time. "You are, then, accusing my client of hiring or ordering the murder of this Norten person?"

"Of course not. We are merely explaining how we established motive." He saw what Vanderhaven was doing! "We believe that Mr. Vincent always was under orders of a higher ... power. One of those higher power people is under arrest and may possibly serve life in federal penitentiary."

"No!" Vincent cried. "I didn't receive orders from anywhere on that! I certainly didn't order or even suggest Norten should be hit! I don't believe he was!"

Judge Vernon rapped his gavel and instructed defense to control their client.

"May we pursue one thing here?" Vanderhaven said, with a short smirk toward Rick. "You said, quite clearly, that you didn't receive orders from anywhere *on that*. What about the women?"

"They were a threat to, I mean, about, the car. And that."

"But you did order that?"

"For god's sake, *shut up!"* Tilton screeched.

Vincent looked shocked. You could see him deflate. It was obvious he would be convicted about the drugs. He would probably be convicted for hiring or ordering two murders.

The rest of the trial was short and foregone. The three attorneys were wishing they'd never heard the name, Phillip Vincent, before it was over.

He was sentenced to life without parole on the drug charges. The murder charges were left in pending. If he were to get out on some technicality or something he would be immediately arrested and tried for murder through conspiracy and receive another life without parole sentence. There is no limitation statute on murder.

And Then

A group of musicians and cops sat around the little table on Emerald Meadow, reminiscing about earlier times and catching up on the latest gossip or whatever.

"It's been two years since this case," Det. Rick Gordon said. "Gangermann is still appealing little technical points. Lawyers have milked him for about twenty million, which he won't miss, even if he does eventually get out."

"Yeah," Randy White replied. "I came back at the two year anniversary to see how things are doing here. I hear Glenda and Luke got married last month. They've opened an agency together. Not many surprise me, but he did.

"How's your love life?"

"I'm seriously considering marrying Annette if she'll have me. (He hugged her.) We get along very well. The problem would be that she's manager of one of the most popular groups in the country. She doesn't have to go to all the shows anymore, so we'll have a lot of time together. *Horror Hiway* is another hit. That makes four singles to top the charts and four platinum CDs.

"Has the drug highway been shut down or is there only a short detour?"

"Great!" Ralph Manners cried. He grabbed his guitar

and went to sit at the next table and strum some power chords.

They talked about anything that came up and ate a very good picnic lunch. Ralph came to sit at the table to ask what they thought of this one. "I call it *Drug Hiway Shutdown*."

It was a sort of heavy metal thing with some power country overtones.

"What do you think?"

"Oh, probably no more than gold," Randy said.

"Platinum. Definitely," Annette decided. "Number three for six weeks international."

"Won't make it above four on the charts," Ginger said.

"Vote with Ginger," Shirley Sanders insisted. "I'm only wrong about that kind of thing eighty percent of the time."

"That will make two in a row with Hiway in the title. A specialty CD with Hiway themes. Call it *Detours*," Randy said.

They played and teased for awhile, then went their separate ways. They would meet there again in two years to see if Gangermann was still appealing his case.

For now, life would get back to as close to normal as it ever did for that bunch.

C. D. Moulton's works are available on most major outlets as printed or e-books. CD writes the CD Grimes, PI, mysteries, the Det. Lt. Nick Storie mysteries, the Clint Faraday mysteries, the Flight of the Maita science fiction series, books on orchid culture and many others of many types. Mystery, adventure, intrigue, science fiction, humor, fantasy, paranormal, mild erotica, and factual.

www.ingramcontent.com/pod-product-compliance
Lightning Source LLC
LaVergne TN
LVHW010502160826
845677LV00012B/2612

* 9 7 9 8 2 0 1 2 1 8 7 1 3 *